This book belongs to

For 1. Evie, 2. Gracie and 3. Elizabeth
C.F.

This edition published by Parragon in 2013
Parragon
Chartist House
15-17 Trim Street
Bath BA1 1HA, UK
www.parragon.com

Published by arrangement with Gullane Children's Books
185 Fleet Street, London, EC4A 2HS

ISBN 978-1-4723-1990-6

Printed in China

Charles Fuge's

Wonderful Wildlife
123

PaRRagon

Bath · New York · Singapore · Hong Kong · Cologne · Delhi
Melbourne · Amsterdam · Johannesburg · Shenzhen

1 lonely badger,

2 helpful whales,

3 friendly seabirds,

singing songs and telling tales.

4 froggy eyes,

5 buzzy flies,

6 little tadpoles
watch their mummies
with surprise.

7 hungry birds,

8 worms that wiggle,

9 hyenas see a sight

that makes them laugh and giggle.

10 fearful fruitbats,

11 worried rats,

12 lazy meerkats,
using rats and bats as mats!

13 ants encourage...

14 naughty moths,

15 holes have ruined

Mrs Panda's tablecloth.

16 Bigfoot footprints,

17 Yeti tracks,

18 cheeky chipmunks, chucking snowballs at their backs!

19 wise old owls,

20...

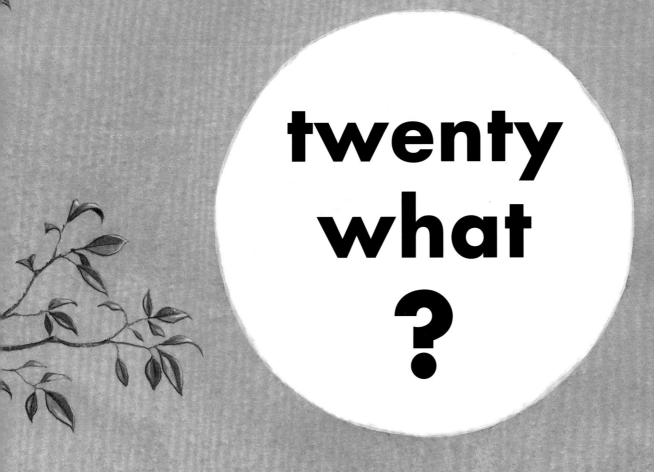

twenty
what
?

That's it now…
that's your lot!